BEDTIME FOR BABY SLOTH

by DANIELLE MCLEAN   Illustrated by

tiger tales

High up in the treetops, Mommy Sloth called to her baby, "Time for bed, little one!"

But Baby Sloth was too busy playing!

"Mommy," Baby Sloth laughed, "I can't go to bed yet. I haven't said good night to the stars and the moon."

Mommy Sloth smiled. "How could I forget! Okay, you can say your good nights. But then it's bedtime. Little sloths need their rest."

Together the sloths looked up at the shimmering sky.
"Good night moon," beamed Baby Sloth.
"Good night stars," added Mommy. "Now come
on, little one. It's bedtime for Baby Sloth."

"But Mommy, I can't go to sleep yet. We haven't sung to the birds. They need their lullaby, or THEY won't be able to sleep," explained Baby Sloth.

"Well, we can't have that!" replied Mommy Sloth, laughing.

So Mommy and Baby Sloth cuddled up together and sang a soft lullaby to the birds as they swooped through the sky.

All was quiet and still when suddenly, Baby Sloth's belly rumbled.

"Mommy, I think I need a bedtime snack," giggled Baby Sloth.

"Just one piece of fruit," answered Mommy Sloth, leaning back so Baby Sloth could pick a juicy one. "The sun is rising, and that means bedtime for baby sloths!"

Baby Sloth was too busy hanging
from a branch and STILL wasn't
ready to sleep.

"Oh, dear! What can we do to settle
you down?" asked Mommy Sloth.
"How about a bedtime story?"

"Yes, please!" smiled Baby Sloth,
climbing down.

While Mommy told the story, Baby Sloth cuddled up
on Mommy's belly and gave a big, stretchy yawn.
    "You're the best at telling stories," sighed Baby Sloth.

    And just as Mommy was reaching the end,
Baby Sloth whispered, "Mommy, I think I'm ready to . . ."

"Sleep?" finished Mommy,
with a kiss on the cheek.

As the sun rose above the horizon, Mommy Sloth
wished Baby Sloth the sweetest of dreams.

"Sleep tight, sleepyhead," she sighed.
And the two sloths dozed happily, all day long.

Did you know that sloths are mostly **nocturnal**? That means they sleep during the day and are awake at night.